Disney *fairies*

# TinkerBell

# Talented Tink

By Andrea Posner-Sanchez
Illustrated by the Disney Storybook Artists

Random House 🏠 New York

Copyright © 2010 Disney Enterprises, Inc. All rights reserved. Published in the United States by Random House Children's Books, a division of Random House, Inc., 1745 Broadway, New York, NY 10019, and in Canada by Random House of Canada Limited, Toronto, in conjunction with Disney Enterprises, Inc. Random House and the colophon are registered trademarks of Random House, Inc.
Library of Congress Control Number: 2009924720
ISBN: 978-0-7364-2655-8
www.randomhouse.com/kids
MANUFACTURED IN CHINA
10 9 8 7 6 5 4 3 2

Every fairy in Pixie Hollow has a special talent. There are garden fairies, water fairies, light fairies, tinker fairies, and fast-flying fairies.

When Tinker Bell first arrived, she didn't know what her talent was.

Queen Clarion had a fairy from each talent group place an object on a magical toadstool. The water fairy brought a drop of water, the garden fairy brought a flower, the fast-flying fairy brought a whirlwind, and the tinker fairy brought a hammer.

"They will help you find your talent," the queen explained to Tinker Bell.

Tink approached each object, waiting to see what would happen. The water droplet burst, the flower faded, and the whirlwind disappeared.

Just when Tink was getting discouraged, the hammer began to glow—and it flew right into her hands!

Everyone cheered. Tinker Bell was a tinker fairy.

Like all tinkers, Tinker Bell is great at fixing stuff. But she also likes
to collect Lost Things and use them to make new inventions.

Tink used a metal wheel and a thimble to create a machine that crushed dozens of berries at once to make berry paint.

She used a harmonica to fashion a super-duper seed collector.

Wherever and whenever Tink finds Lost Things, she stops in her tracks and starts tinkering. Once, she found an old porcelain box on the beach, along with a bunch of springs, coils, and gears.

Tinker Bell's friends watched in amazement as she expertly fit all the odds and ends together. What was she making?

It was a beautiful music box!
Tinker Bell isn't just a tinker fairy—she's
the most talented tinker in all of Pixie Hollow!

# TinkerBell
### AND THE
## LOST TREASURE

# Terrific Terence

By Andrea Posner-Sanchez
Illustrated by the Disney Storybook Artists

Random House 🏠 New York

Library of Congress Control Number: 2009924720
ISBN: 978-0-7364-2655-8
www.randomhouse.com/kids
MANUFACTURED IN CHINA
10 9 8 7 6 5 4 3 2

© Disney

Terence has a very important job: he is a dust-keeper fairy. He is in charge of delivering a precise amount of pixie dust to each fairy, every day. Without pixie dust, the fairies can't fly.
Terence is terrific at what he does.

Terence's best friend is Tinker Bell. He always brings her
Lost Things for her inventions. This big stretchy band will be
part of Tink's new boat.

Terence is terrific at finding just what Tink needs.

Sometimes, Tink's inventions don't work out the way she likes. This makes her very angry. But Terence always knows how to cheer her up.

"Ah, it just needs a little more tinkering. Now, who do I know who's a good tinkerer?" Terence jokes. Tinker Bell can't help chuckling.

Terence is terrific at making his friend laugh.

When Tinker Bell is selected to create the Autumn Scepter, Terence knows she will need to spend all her time working. He arrives at Tink's house bright and early the next morning with a delicious breakfast to start her day off right.

Terence is terrific at delivering tasty treats.

While Tinker Bell works on the scepter, Terence takes care of her house. He sweeps the floor, dusts her tools, and starts a fire in the fireplace.

Terence is terrific at keeping things neat and tidy.

When Tinker Bell needs a wish granted and goes off in search of the enchanted Mirror of Incanta, she finds herself in real danger. Luckily, Terence shows up and swings her to safety.
Terence is terrific at coming to the rescue.

Usually, Tink likes to tinker by herself. But she realizes there is only one way to get the scepter done in time for the Autumn Revelry—she asks Terence to help.

Terence is terrific at helping.

Terence is proud of Tinker Bell as she presents the finished scepter for all of Pixie Hollow to see.

Terence is terrific at supporting his friend.

Terence is terrific! And he thinks Tinker Bell is pretty terrific, too!